SEX and LOVE in a Covenant Marriage

Know and learn thirty-nine ways of sex expressions to raise temperatures in your bedroom, and how to season and flavour Love

Published by New Generation Publishing in 2018

First Edition

www.newgeneration-publishing.com

Contents

Introduction: Love and Sex the foundation of an excellent marriage 1

Chapter 1: Thirty-Nine Love Expressions of Love 3

Chapter 2: Foods that Stimulate the Sex Hormones 43

Chapter 3: More Important Scriptures to a Marriage Covenant Partnership 44

Introduction

"Let him kiss me with the kisses of his mouth, for your love is better than wine, because of the fragrance of your good ointments, your name is ointment poured forth."

– Song of Solomon 1:1-4

Have you ever wondered if regular sex plays an important role in marriage, or if you should plan and prepare for it mentally, physically, emotionally and spiritually? In this part of the book, I explain, teach and show you thirty-nine ways of sex expressions that will stimulate, pleasure and hot up temperatures in your love making. Each position has a name to introduce: fun, pleasure, excitement, laughter, enjoyment, character and bonding sessions.

Sex and love is for better and for worse in a covenant marriage. This means that both husband and wife play a very important role in a marriage. Husband, as the head of the house. As head he is the provider of the family, he makes sure that everything is in order spiritually and naturally. I Corinthians 14:40 tells that let all things be decently and in order. A good husband does not take advantage of his position, as head of the house, he does not disrespect his wife, abuse her emotionally, physically or verbally.

Being head does mean bossing your family around, making them feel inferior. A good head supports, cares, nurtures his family, protects, and listens to them; he cares more about making sure his family is happy. It is not about coming in and demanding food to be on the table, ordering the wife around, talking down to her. The wife's role is equally important, it is a partnership that requires both parties to work together for it to work. Matthew 12:25 says, *"Every kingdom divided against itself is brought to desolation, and every city or house divided against itself will not stand."* Matthew 7:18 says, *"A good tree cannot bear bad fruit, nor can a bad tree bear good fruit."* In a marriage a good husband will produce a good wife and a bad husband will produce a bad wife, for the women, Proverbs 14:1 tells that, *"The wise woman builds her house, but the foolish pulls it down with her hands."*

For foundation of an excellent marriage, it is very important that the foundation of your marriage is founded on the word of God. A good marriage consists of God as the centre of the marriage, underneath husband and wife. It is vital that we understand the word of God concerning our role as stewards. Ephesians 5:25 instructs that husbands should love their wives, just as Christ also loved the church, so husbands ought to love their own wives as their own bodies – he who loves his wife loves himself. In the book of I Peter 3:1: *"Wives are instructed, to likewise, be submissive to your own husband, that even if some do not obey the word, they without a word, may be won by the conduct of their wives, a good wife/husband understands the importance of being submissive to each other."*

Chapter 1

Thirty-Nine Love Expressions of Love

Your lips, o my spouse, drip as the honeycomb, honey and milk under your tongue.

This position is a high rising temperature spot allowing your husband to go deep, and puts your wife up the best clitoral stimulation. Together you have control with the rhythm and depth of the smooth riding, so you can take this rhythm from slow all the way up to moving fast. The husband sits in a comfortable chair/bed, wife sits in front on his lap, facing him with her knees bent and placed on either side of his hips. Each have free hands to explore touching in new ways and feeling how much you are enjoying what you do to each other.

I sleep, but my heart is awake, it is the voice of my beloved, he knocks saying, open for me my love.

Take charge of controlling the rhythm and speed of your adventure; change positions – husband sits on the bed with his legs open in front of him, while the wife sits between his legs, facing him with her knees up and her feet outside of his hips. Together you lean back on your hands as your eyes meet, face-to-face out of reach just close to gently kiss, looking eye-to-eye, as this creates an extremely bonding experience. Watch your husband/wife; this hot spot stimulates the emotions arousing reactions – respond by touching and feeling each other.

The fragrance of your breath like apples and the roof of your mouth like the best fruit wine.

When God made the penis and the vagina, He made a perfect match. This position allows her to lie on her side, top leg bent and rolled down to the bed in front of her. He places himself between her legs and enters her, his hands behind her back, he has easy access to slide right in. However, if he stays too long in this position it can be challenging on the lock and could cause strain in the back and shoulders, so have some aromatherapy oils for a deep message afterwards.

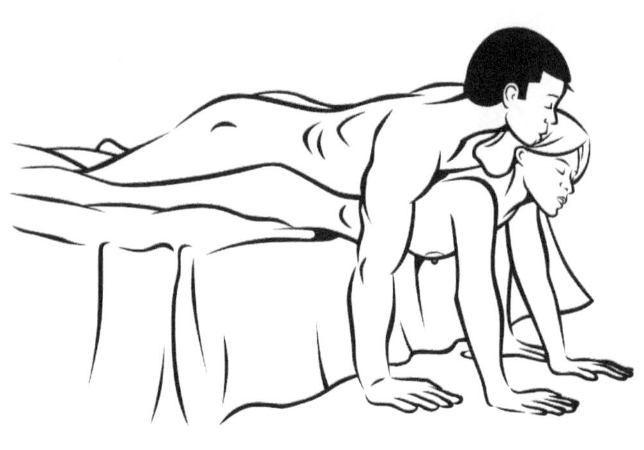

Moving gently the lips of sleepers.

In this position you are making love holding each other very close with the sides of your faces touching, so you can gently and softly talk or sing romantic songs/words to each other. Because your contact is so close, you can feel and act sexy; you can even move from the bed to the floor in your rhythm. Let her lie on the bed, with top body off the bed supporting her arms, while he places himself between her legs, then spreads out on top of her legs, and then lays out on top of her, putting his hands on the floor next to hers. This position works because he supports most of his weight on his arms, so her rib cage is not pressed beneath him. For intense pleasure give your rhythm some power and ride; if you want her to slide forward, you can press her calves down with your ankles. You can also support yourself against her for even deeper gyrating moves, allow her to use her top body to slide back against him for double climax performance.

This statue of yours is like a palm tree and your breast like its cluster.

Lift your leg up and your upper body using your hands, and let the bottom part of body move to rhythm to control the action; small movements and the tilt of your hips makes a difference to your enjoyment. By him standing on the edge of the bed and her wrapping her arms round him and can lift her legs to the bed, with one foot on either side of him, using his one arm to hold her close to him with the other hand under her thigh to give her a bit more support, allowing her to steady her legs against the bed to raise and lower herself against him standing up. You can use walls if you want, try this position in the place between the bed and wall resting her on the bed, with him leaning back against the wall, together comfortably supported up, giving him strength to keep going for longer, deeper rhythms reaching the right spot.

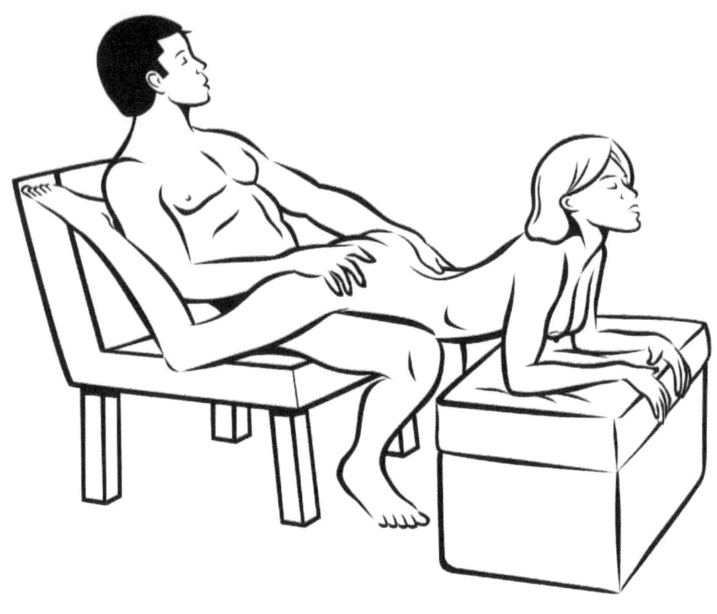

Turn your eyes away from me for they have overcome me,
your hair is like a flock of goats

For the woman who loves the top position and the man who enjoys the back seat view of the booty, in this position you are both able to move each other to the right beat, flowing together and getting maximum pleasure. For more intense fun, the man can sit back in the chair so he can see her sit on him with her legs apart, leaning front bring her legs back, hold firm her arms on the bed, allowing her to take control of the speed and movements; for him it's time to enjoy and see in full view the booty, him sitting down doesn't mean she has to do all the work, he can assist her hips and thighs as she rides him or even massages her back.

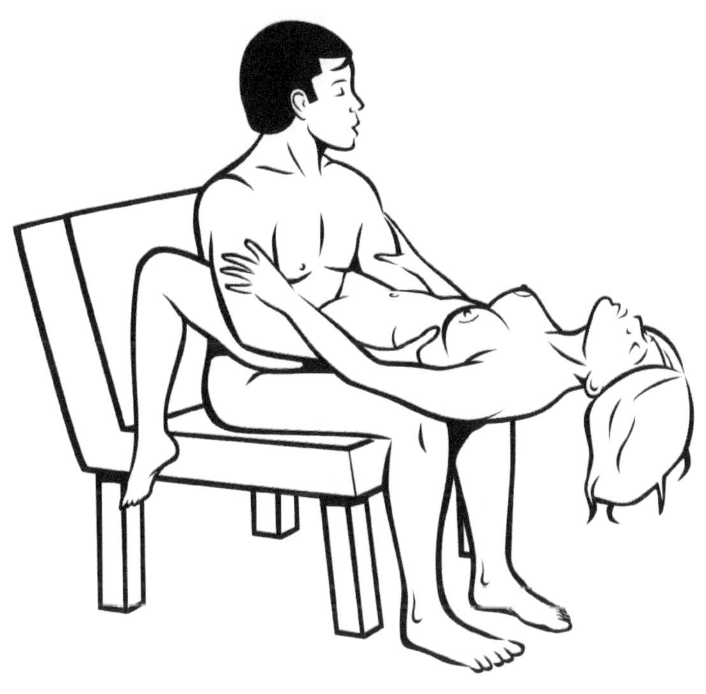

Every one bears twins and none is barren among them.

He sits in a chair, while she sits on him with her legs apart and lies back to rest her back flat on his knees, scooped up and close to him. In this spot he can reach deep penetration from teasing up against his lower stomach. He can put one hand on her breast and the other on her clitoris; these combinations are very pleasurable and bonding.

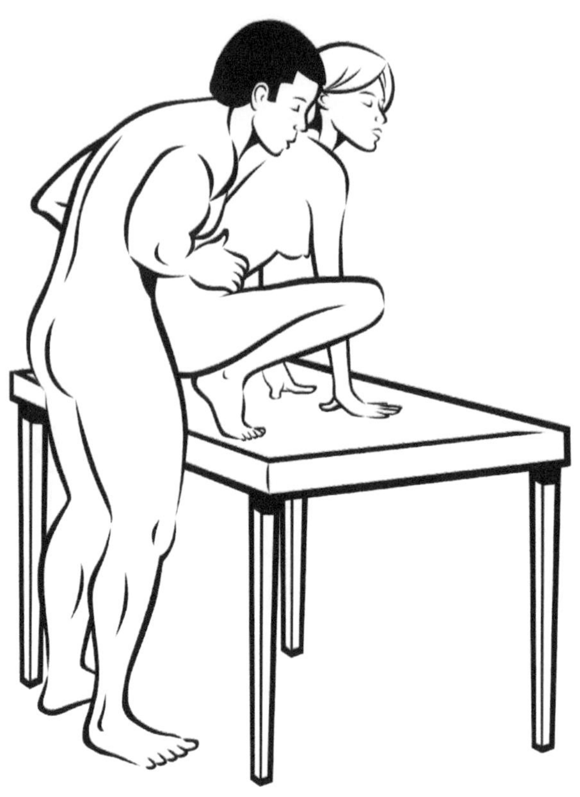

I have taken off my robe; how can I put it on again? I have washed my feet, how can I defile them?

Honour for the woman. This position allows the special woman to feel celebrated; she gets on a high surface as in the picture, facing away couching down with her legs spread open, he places her hands in front of her to stay supported, him standing upright, and his pelvis should be at a perfect spooning spot with her booty, insert his penis, both begin to move to rhythm. In this squatting position you can create better vaginal penetration, also using his energy to move her hips up and down, kissing her neck and back, or massaging her clitoris and breasts, loving from behind. In all, labour has its rewards.

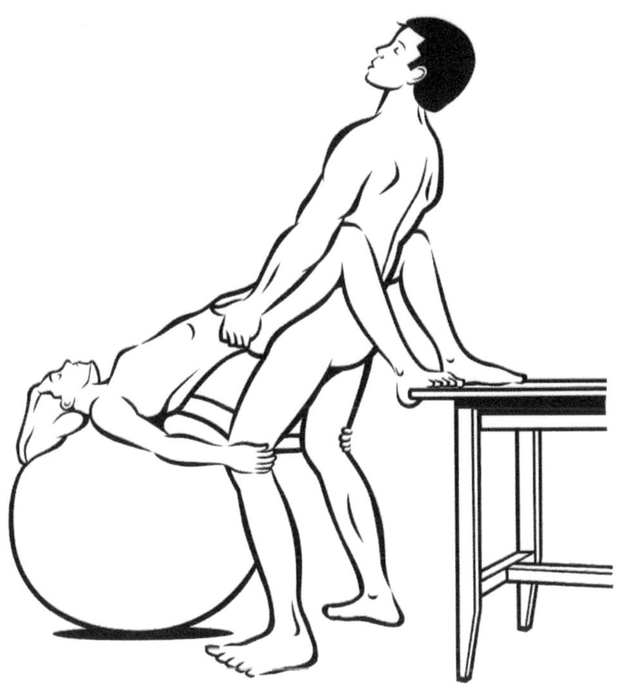

Until the day breaks and the shadows flee away.

Creative acrobatic sex is fun, try using an exercise ball, with this position she lies back on the exercise ball with her head, neck and upper part of the body supported on the ball, she lifts her lower part to his pelvis and holds onto her, she places her feet on a high chair behind him, the support of her feet will give her power to have some fun and enjoyment. Try changing positions back to front and front to back.

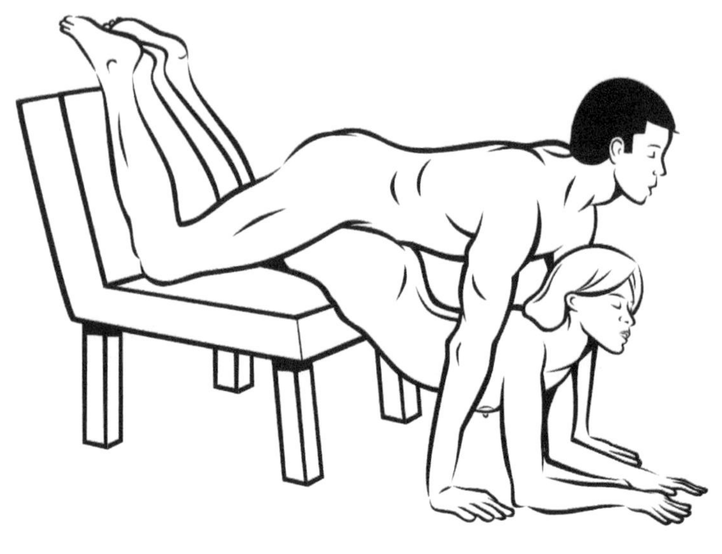

I sat down in his shade with great delight. And his fruit sweet to my taste.

Hot up with this bow-wow-style position. Facing away and down she rests her hips on the edge of a chair (as seen the picture), while her arms position her body on the ground, supporting himself directly on top of her, his arms over her shoulders, his legs and hers should be bent against the back of the chair. Take special care in this position; the higher the chair, the more strain there may be, however, the downward angle of her pelvis will allow him to insert himself from above and behind her, and the sloping position will allow for deeper penetration.

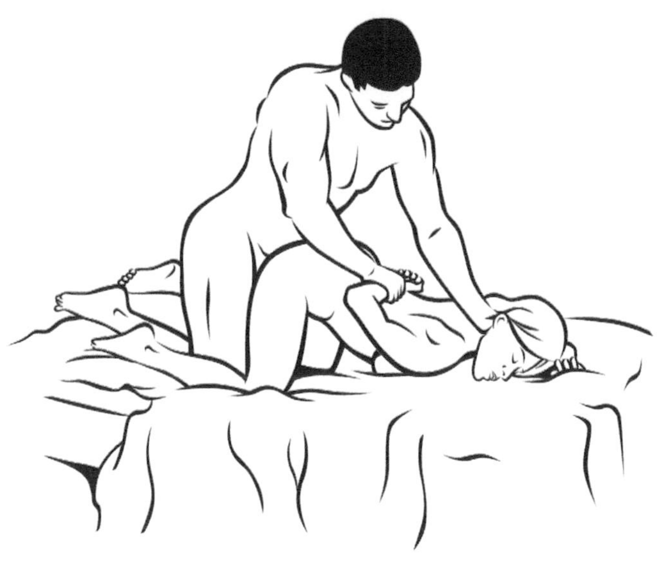

He brought me to the banqueting house and his banner over me was love.

The husband leads in this position, kneeling on the bed, he carries her in his arms, her back should be sloping over the top of the bed, while he gently holds her lower back and hips against his pelvis. Extended upwards her legs should comfortably rest against his chest, so that her feet are just above his head, the back of the chair will support her and her hips high, so he can use his best power penis muscles against her. If she holds on tight, he can use a free hand to rub her clitoris, tease her nipples or run his hands through her hair, keeping her legs straight and together will keep things nice and tight for each other.

I have eaten my honeycomb with my honey.

In this position she kneels on the bed and he kneels behind her. He pushes her shoulder down on the bed while gently turning her arm behind her back, he then enters her from behind, even though she looks disarmed, she can still move her hips to meet his rides, he can use his grip on her to help him move deeper.

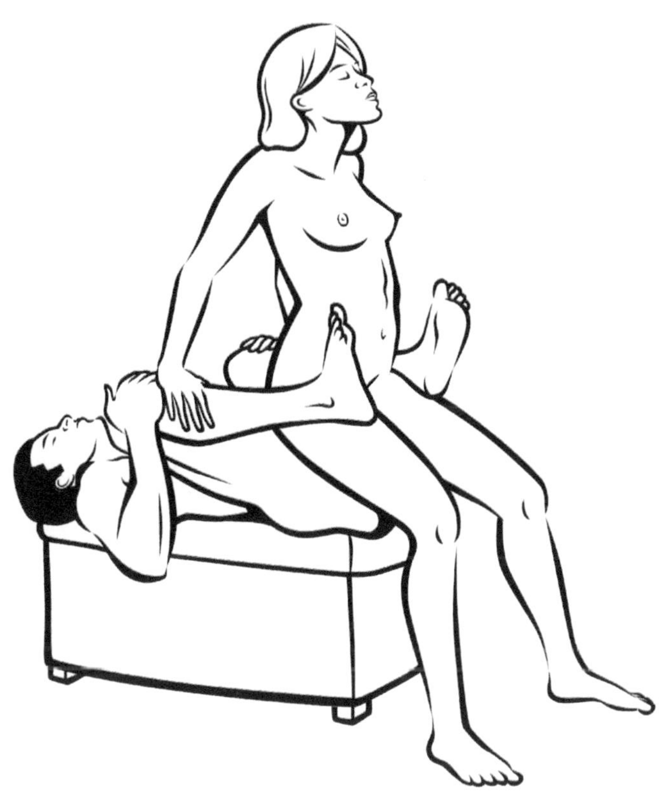

The curves of your high are like jewels.

In this classic position, she moves it slowly about 90 degrees clockwise; the back entry position allows her to control the speed, rhythm and depth of their rides. Using her legs for support, he lies back on a bed or chair and draws his knees up to his chest. She positions herself between his legs, facing out as she lowers herself onto him, he can rest his heels on her thighs to support her and pull her closer. The tight fit of angle allows her to move herself back and forth, fast or slow to rhythm.

On the handles of the lock.

The upper strength of him and her is key in this position. She places her hands flat on a comfortable bed or chair, and he stands behind her and slowly lifts her to his hips while she supports her upper body in a push upward move. As he enters her she wraps her legs around his body for additional support; this can be a tricky position, but if you do master it, it's very enjoyable.

His legs are pillars of marble.

In this position, use the bed as it is more comfortable or chair if you desire. He sits upside down in the chair, facing up, his legs should be bent with his feet resting on the seat back, she floats over him just above his head so that he is in range of a hot clitoral kissing session, she should lean over him hugging his upper thighs to steady herself while she performs oral stimulation on him. Each partner will have free hands for extras, to either for him to stimulate her clitoris or love her or she can use her hand to play with his balls, the flow of blood to his head will be a whole new and exciting sensation for him. Prepare for this position by cleaning all body parts thoroughly, and have an over body scrub and then apply some scented body oil or body lotion.

As a seal upon your arm.

Simple and effortless, he lies on the bed on his back while she climbs on top facing his feet, she slides onto his penis make sure that you are feeling comfortable and relaxed, she lifts and crosses her legs until she is sitting on his hips, he supports her hips with his hands to help her balance.

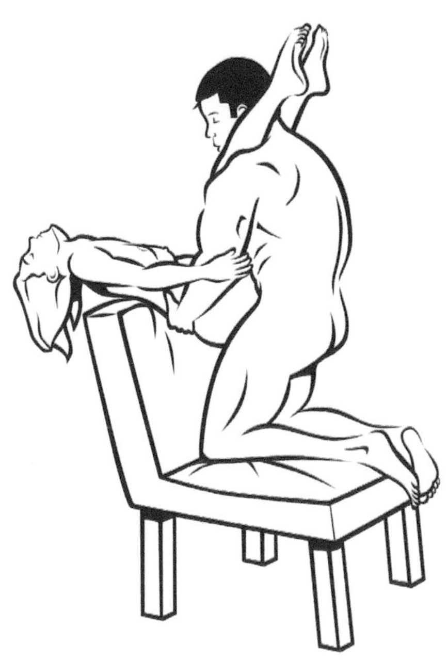

Take hold of its branches.

For all the husbands who love booty-shaking, this is for you. Start by entering from the back, with your hips resting on the bed, and focus your moves on long, slow rides instead of fast ones. The result is a deliciously slow burning ride. Be dynamic with your moves from a different angle; she lies face down, propped up on her elbows with her legs open, he is in the push-upward position behind her, his legs on the inside of hers as he leans forward, she supports her back resting her head under his chin, she bends her knees to wrap her legs around his butt. Put a pillow or a cushion beneath her hips to lift her pelvis and to create more comfort. Penetrate in this angle, he may be on top, she should assist in the movements of rides and speed of the rhythm, she can use her legs around his bottom to pull him closer, and meet his hips as he moves in this angle, he has room for slow/fast ride, tilting both your hips brings your performance to a climax end.

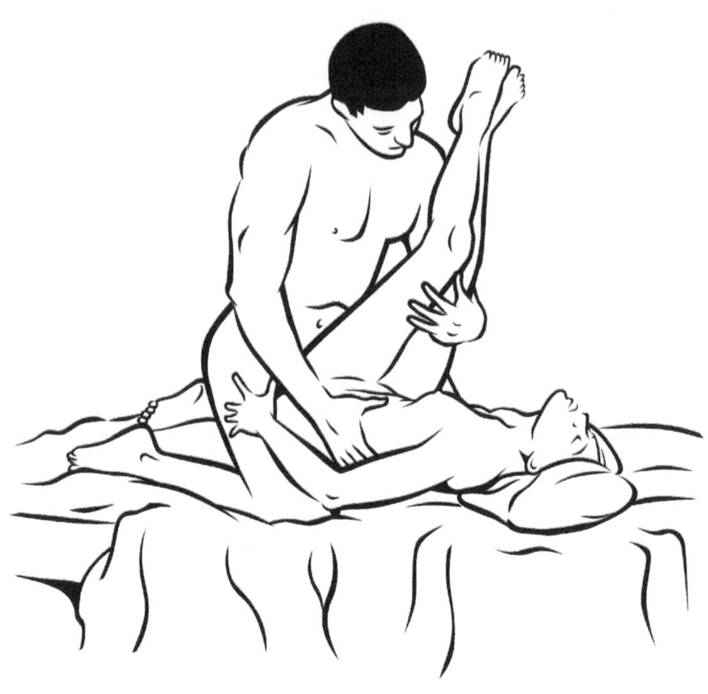

Your waist is a heap of wheat.

If excitement is your thing, this one is for you, from the behind entry as seen, she bends forward giving him a fantastic view of her booty, the tilting of her body helps each riding rhythm the right way, he sits on the bed with his legs straight out in front of him, she sits on his lap with her knees outside her back against his chest, as she slides him inside of her. Once he's in position, she leans forward toward his legs as he helps tuck her legs behind him she slowly spreads further until she is lying face down between his outstretched legs, her hips should be up a bit, resting on his thighs to help get the right moving and riding angle.

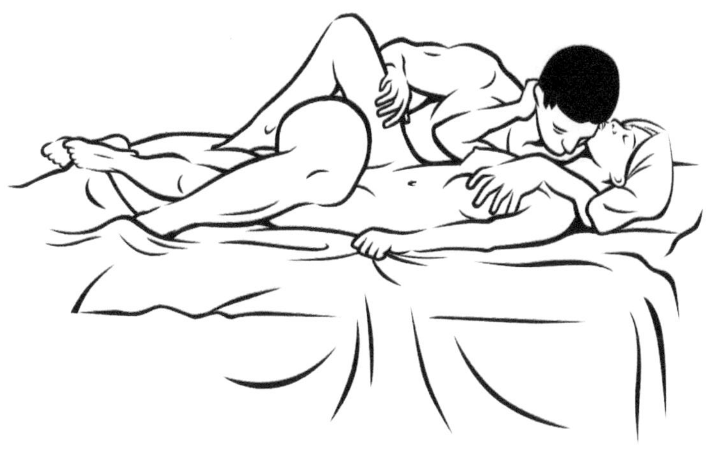

A king is held captive by your tresses.

In this one, she crouches on the bed in the runner's position, with one leg bent into a lunge and the other rolled out straight back, while he positions himself between her open legs. The outstretched leg and knees behind her, she supports her weight on her elbows; he's got plenty of room for movement, and her back leg-front leg position make it an extra tight hug, she can always change legs if she gets exhausted.

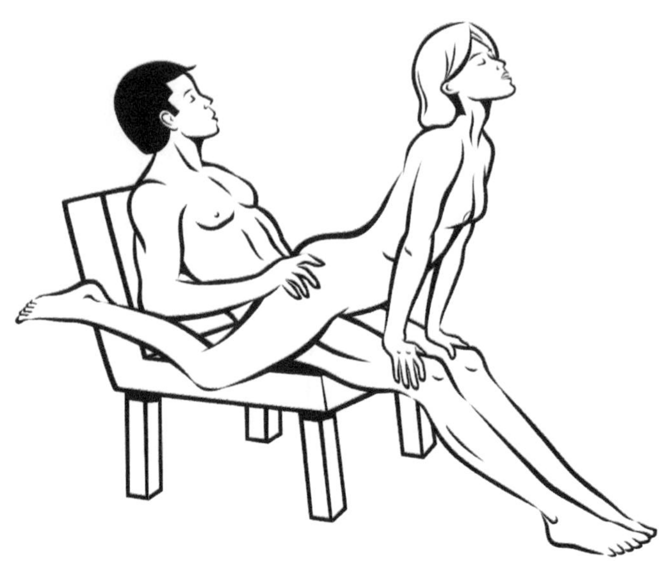

Blow upon my garden.

Good balance is required in this one. She sits in a big chair or bed on his lap facing his feet, and slides onto his penis. She then tucks her legs on either side of the chair or bed as she slowly leans forward resting her hands on his thighs, she supports her back to intense pleasure, this behind entry position has a tight fit and feel, tilting of her hips will gives you both a different kind of sensation, her leaning forward more and more will keep changing the sensations, the more she bends, the more access he has to touch smack or feel her ass.

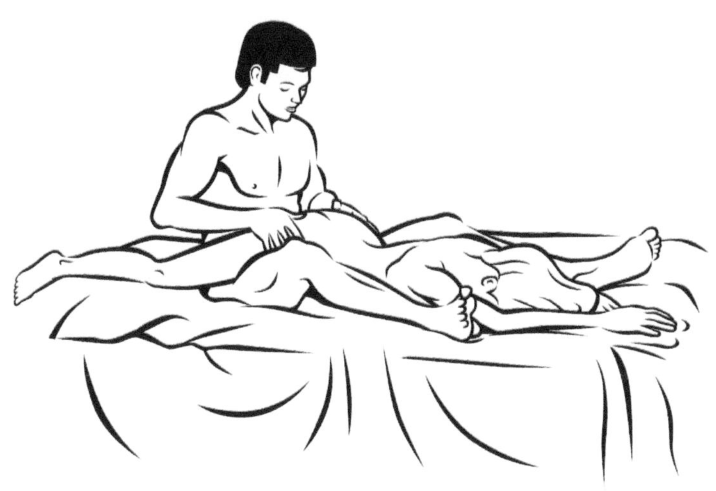

O fairest among women.

Fun is this one, she should turn to lie mostly flat on her front/back, while turning to lie mostly flat on her back/front, while he brings his upper her in between her, her upper leg should be lifted to give enough space for him to insert himself from behind, and her knees should be bent over his leg so that she can use it to make for a slower, more sensual pace, they can both glide along on one other, while her upper body is still lying flat, he can still lean in and nibble at her ears, kiss her neck, using his upper arm to linger a soft hand along her legs, tease her clitoris or hold on to her hips, in the meantime his lower arm can be under her to support her head and the free hand can softly reach out to massage her breast and stomach.

The king has brought me into his chambers.

Watch each other while turning one other in this acrobatic position, as you can see in the picture below in a composed manner for him, she lies down on the bed or floor, he kneels in front of her while she squirts her butt to meet him, both of her legs should be raised, her legs can be bent comfortably out on the bed, which will give him access to her breasts, and the ability to see her facial expressions; keeping her legs in tune makes this one a pleasurable experience and the angle of her raised hips brings the excitement deeper inside her.

Like a piece of pomegranate, are your temple behind your veil.

Trying a new sex angle is interesting and fun. You both should lie down on the bed parallel to one another, facing the same side of the room, as seen in the picture, he should enter her from behind and, if necessary, her body can be angled in a slight 'L' in order to let him in more easily. This move stays at a slow, sensual ride, where both partners can caress and tease one another, working up to a low, long climax, he can tease her clitoris and she can reach a hand between his legs to massage his balls.

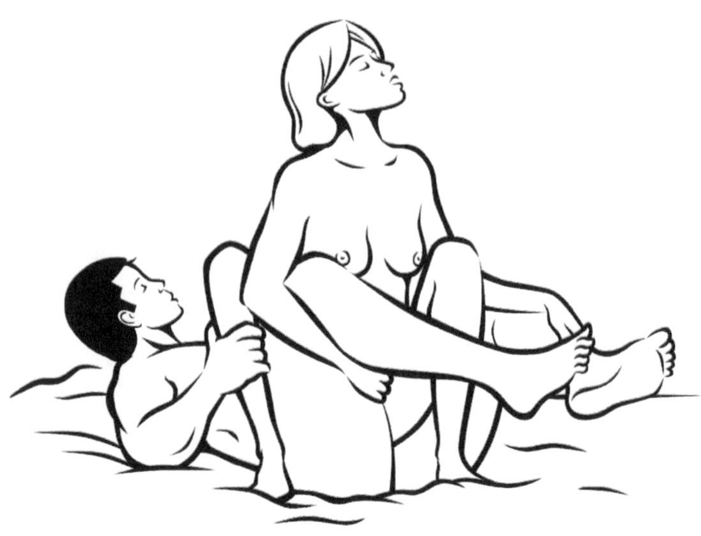

My beloved put his hand by the latch of the door and my heart yearned for him.

In this move you need either a comfortable bed or chair or floor, putting his penis in from upside down, giving her some foreplay will make it a lot easier for him to slip in when it's time to get rolling. She should sit back in a comfortable bed/floor, with her legs extended, he should enter her facing away using the support in front of him, the bed works best here, so that his legs can lie flat behind it, she should keep her legs as seen in the picture, he faces his pelvis down and forward, he goes in, once this has happened it's lot easier to move to a nice and slow rhythm, and both get to feel and enjoy from a whole new angle.

Behold you are handsome my beloved, yes pleasant, also our bed is green.

The exercise position, because it will help tone those muscles in the penis and vagina keeps everything else fit and in good shape. In this position she lies upright across a bed, she should bring her knees to her chest to make room for him, he squats down facing away and angles his hips forward so that he can enter her from above, she can rest her legs on his shoulder, pleasuring position for her and will also keep things hot and tight for him. This position is particularly exciting because his penis is upside down, the plump down_of this move will awake all sensitive parts different from the usual position, and with this fun angle he will also surprise her with a wonderful ride of pressure from his balls on her clitoris as he rides away.

Behold you are handsome, my beloved yes, pleasant, also our bed is green.

Use the upper body strength from him and some leg extensions from her. She should lie on her side on the edge of the bed, so that her hips come to the edge, he stands at the edge of her legs, so that her toes point to the ceiling, he should take hold of her thigh and bring it close to his chest so that her leg extends beyond his shoulders with his other hand, he can support her bum or hips. She should use her elbows to keep her body lifted off the bed, her other leg should be comfortably folded in between his legs, she should use her arms to push up from the bed, every time he pulls her up in a romantic ride. This position requires some upper body strength from both partners, but is worth it because of how deeply he can penetrate her; it explores the sideways entry position.

A bundle of myrrh is my beloved to me.

She lies down on the bed/floor, her knees to her chest, her feet should be up in the air, but they don't need to be spread far apart, instead of lying directly on top of her, he should angle himself upright over her so that he enters her facing to the side, allowing you both a tight fit closely inside, by tightening her thighs together, she can continue to alter the sensation by leaning her closed legs to one or another. This position gives him creative control over the speed and rhythm of the experience, while she gets to lie back and feel him work.

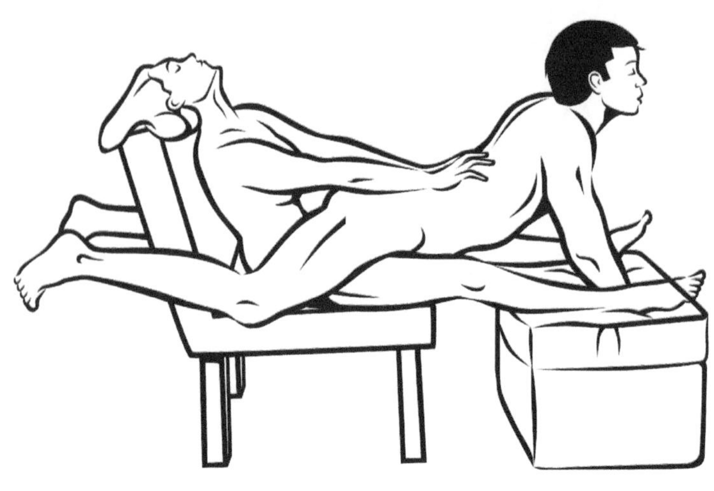

The time of singing has come, and the voice of the turtledove.

She lies down on the bed, with him on his knees directly in front of her, she should cross her legs so that her right foot rests on his right shoulder and her left foot rests on his left shoulder. He can hold on to either her ankles or knees to keep her in place; she can cross her legs by her shins, or for a tighter fit, cross above the knee, changing where her legs are crossed throughout. This passionate session will keep things exciting and hot. In this angle, both husband and wife are able to watch each other work as things get really flavoured up, though he is controlling in this position, she doesn't have to lie back doing nothing, she can tighten her pelvis muscles arousing his penis intensely.

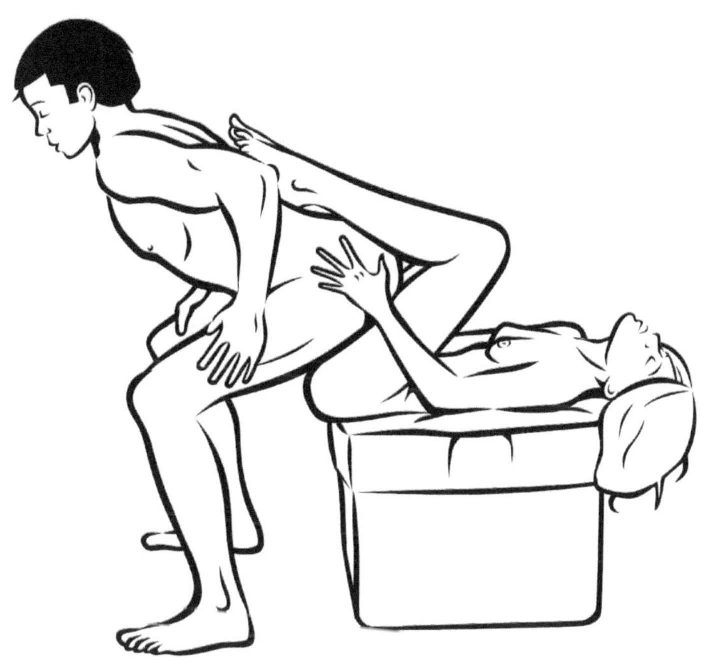

Let me hear your voice for your voice is sweet.

She lies down on the bed with his knees up and feet raised slightly in the air, she faces away squirting down over his pelvis with her feet flat on the bed and her knees up. Instead of keeping both of her feet in between his legs, she should have one leg between his legs and the other extended over his right leg or left if she is on the left; her hips should face the thigh, she is extended because his legs are secured a little bit off the bed, his upper thigh will touch lightly her clitoris, he has free hands to either slide herself up and down, and massage his balls, in this angle both can feel the depth of the penetration.

Its support of gold, its seat of purple, and its interior paved with love.

If regular a 69 is boring for you, try this version, which has more flexibility from her, so make sure she extends first. He lies down on the bed and raises his legs in the air, as parallel to her own head as possible, holding on to the back of her hips (as seen in the picture), he should kneel over her so that his penis is accessible to her mouth, without her having to do much of anything with his arm on either side of her hips, he should be face to face. Good position if you want some diversity.

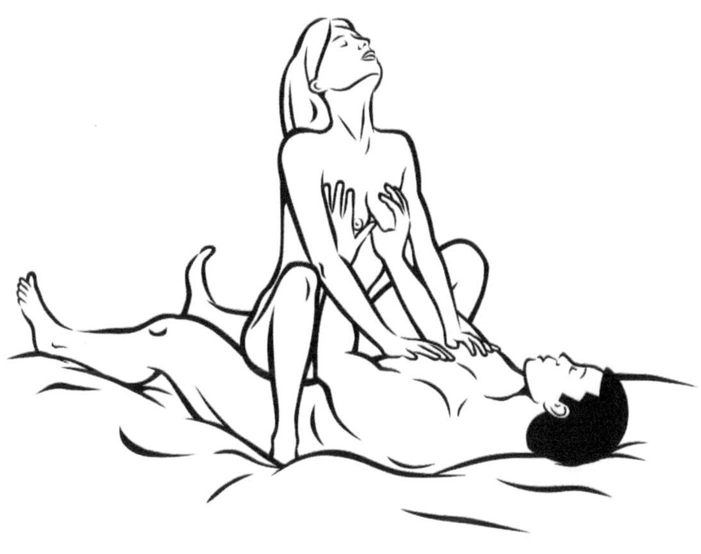

Built for an armoury on which hangs a thousand buckles.

Him lying on the bed, she gets on top of him, she should spread open her legs for him to enter her, she should turn out her legs in the air into a wide split, straightening her all the way, he should keep her apart by holding on to her breasts for a wide split or her knees for a thinner split, when he is riding to rhythm in between her legs, creating a much needed bonding session for both partners.

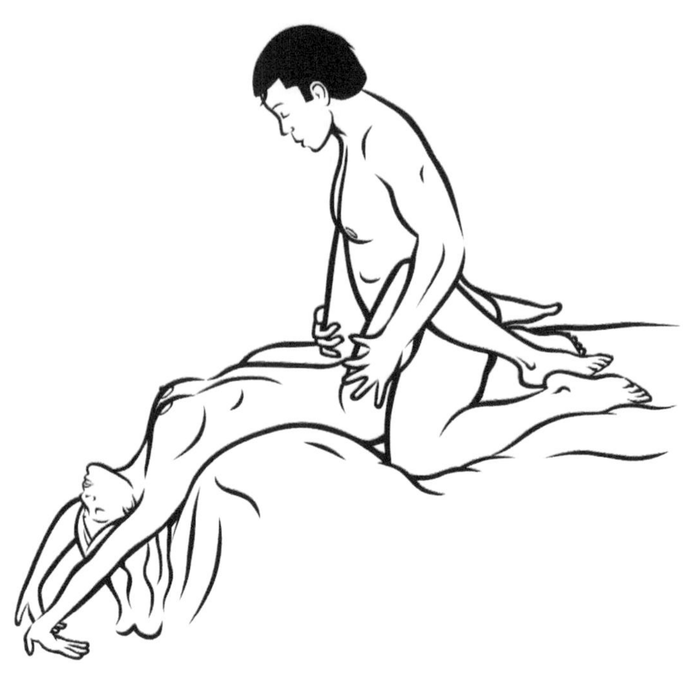

He brought me to the banqueting house and his banner over me was love.

She lies on her back with her knees closely on her chest, he kneels in front of her where he is most comfortable moving in for pleasure, instead of extending her legs out or wrapping her ankles around his head, this position just asks that she put her feet flat on his chest. She aims to have her big toes touching her big toes and her heels touching her heels, the closer her feet are together, the tighter he will fit inside of her, she can practise flexing her pelvis muscles so that the tightening around his penis will expand and contract, giving him a rhythm to work with as he goes in and out of her. Doing this feels good for him and for her, moving the pelvis muscles will make give a very pleasurable climax.

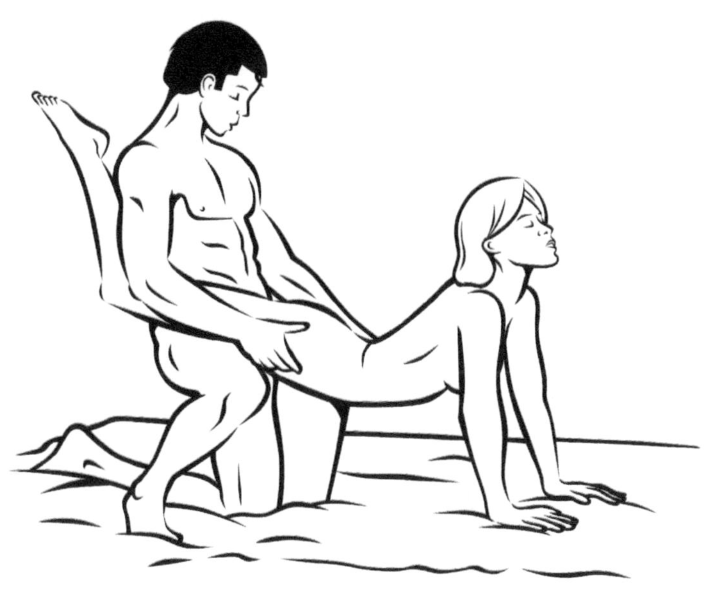

Refresh me with apples, for I am love sick.

She lies down on the bed with her legs curled up to her chin, he lies down on top of her hovering over her, keeping her knees bent, her ankles are around his neck, the closeness of her feet together, allows a tight so that she is able to fit around him inside her, his weight on top of her will keep her knees close to her chest, giving him greater depth as he moves in and out of her. This position still allows both partners to maintain eye contact throughout and even for him to lean for the occasional passionate kiss. Be careful not to put too much weight on top of her, otherwise her knees will prevent her from breathing comfortably.

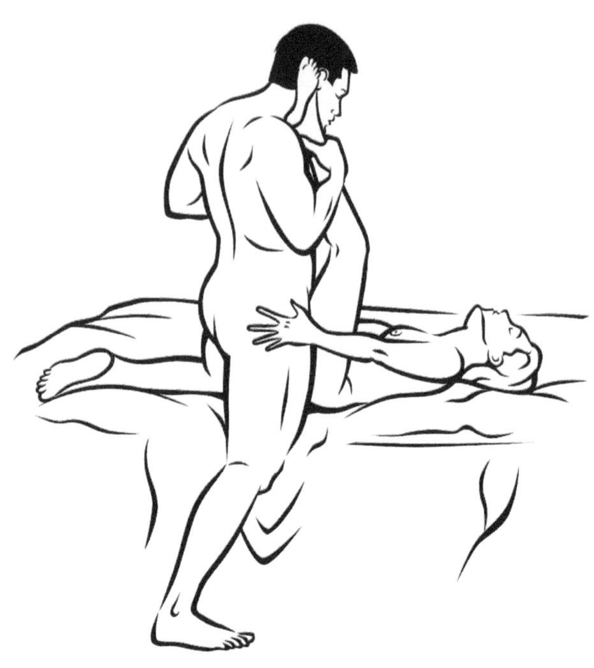

The fig tree puts forth her screen figs and the vines with the tender grapes.

She lies down on the edge of the bed with one or both legs raised, while he stands in front of her, with one leg firmly on the floor and the other on the bed. Holding one of her legs in the air, and the other comfortably to her side, he can enter her deeply, while she can grab his hips to pull him in deeper as he rides.

I sat down in his shade with great delight and his fruit was sweet to my taste.

She arranges herself on all fours, he kneels upright behind her, he should raise one leg so that his foot is resting flat on the bed or floor; she should raise her leg on the same side back and up, so that her thigh rests on top of his and her calf and foot extend comfortably up and behind him using her hips as his lead. To control his rides, she uses her arms in front of her for support with her leg high, to get more of himself inside her, for her to get some clitoral stimulation, he can use this angle to feel her breasts. The style and feel of this position is incredible.

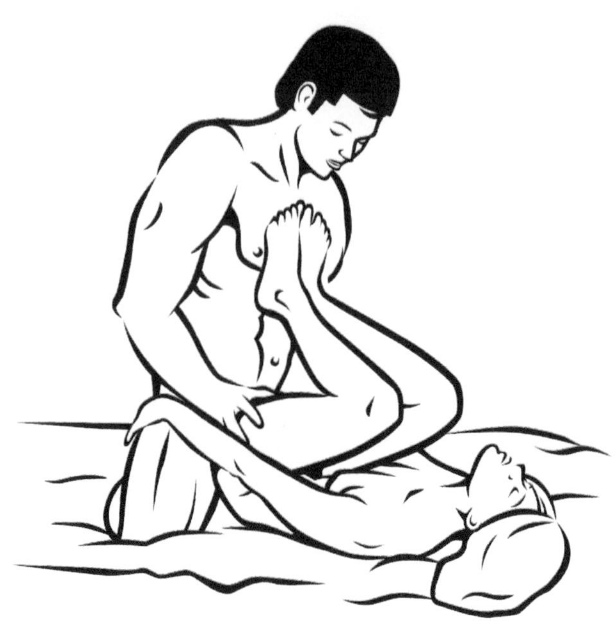

Awake, O north wind, and come, O south blow upon my garden, that its spices may flow out.

She kneels in front of him, squirting herself forward as he inserts himself inside her, doing it naturally, she should let out extending her arms off the bed and touching her fingertips along the floor like shown in the picture. He can help her reach the floor by moving her hips, keeping herself on the bed, he is able to view her stomach and chest as she loosens up her body. Nice way to start your morning, his positioning right in front of her open hips is good for some pleasurable fun, that can be done anytime.

Many waters cannot quench love nor can the floods drown it.

She lies down, she crouches down on top of him with her knees close to her chest, and her feet flat on the bed, using her quad muscles, bringing her pelvis up and down his penis, gently and lightly hovering over the tip, repeat this action to allow her legs to open up, so that she can take in the whole length of his penis, by leaning back slightly the tip of his penis will hot him up with excitement feeling great. He can make use of his hands to massage her breasts, and rub her clitoris, increasing the pleasure.

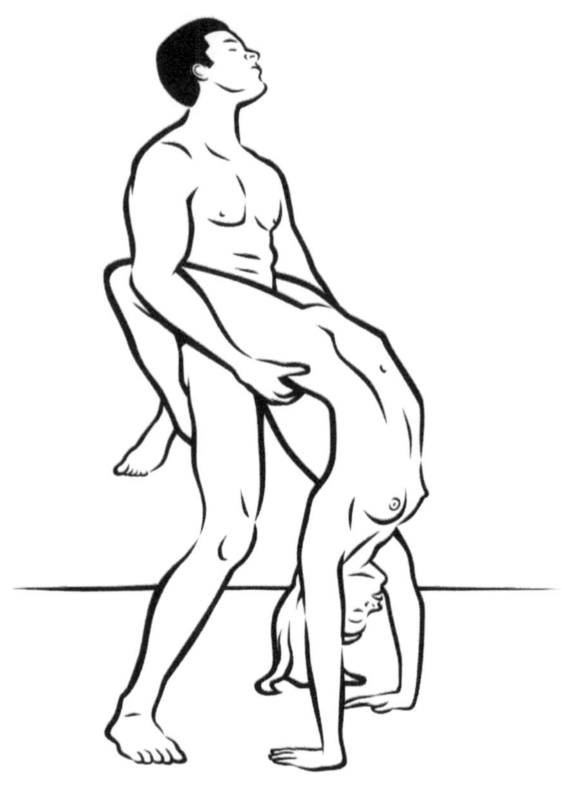

By the rivers of waters washed with milk, and fitly set.

Good balance is required to do this one, strength in the legs will help to stay up, he bench-presses her from below, he lies on the floor with his head propped on a pillow and his feet up high against the wall, she sits on him, pressing her body to his legs and her hands against the wall, she can control the speed and depth of their movements by raising and lowering her hips, holding his ankles for traction if she needs to; he can help by supporting her ass with his free hands, he to view of the workout, persevering at a lower speed allows you to enjoy this one.

Sustain me with cakes of raisins.

Strength, flexibility and balance is crucial for this one, the twisty backward angle gives you a wow factor, he sits wide-legged and holds her thighs around his hips, as she holds on to his neck, when he is inside her, she slowly lowers herself back, until her hands touch the floor, he enters and rides into her as she supports herself with her hands on the floor. Curve your back to try out a diverse angle.

In the secret places of the cliff, let me see your face.

Strong back shoulders and core muscles for this one, so be careful if you have been avoiding the gym. She starts in a push-upward position with her thighs on the bed and her upper body supported by her hands on the floor, he positions himself between her legs, rolls her onto her side, pulling a leg up to his shoulder and supporting her body weight with both hands around her hips. This sideways position gives you a nice tight feel, when you are to remain upright, with his two feet on the ground, he is in control in this move, if you prefer rough ride or rhythm moves that are very wild, this position is a good option for both.

Chapter 2

Foods that Stimulate the Sex Hormones

In this chapter, I have made a list of some of the foods that help to stimulate, increase and heighten your sexual desire for each other.

- Almonds
- Linseed
- Asparagus
- Avocados
- Bananas
- Chilies
- Dark Chocolate
- Fish – Omega-3 fatty acids, Vitamin B5, B6 and B12
- Garlic
- Oysters
- Watermelon

Chapter 3

More Important Scriptures to a Marriage Covenant Partnership

"Marriage is honorable among all and the bed undefiled."
– Hebrews 13:4

"When I was a child, I spoke, as a child, I understood as a child I though as a child, but when I became a man, I put away childish things."
– I Corinthians 13:11

"If the salt loses its flavor, how shall it be seasoned?"
– Mathew 5:13

www.ingramcontent.com/pod-product-compliance
Ingram Content Group UK Ltd.
Pitfield, Milton Keynes, MK11 3LW, UK
UKHW042001190726
13854UKWH00005B/2100

9 781789 559132